Mem Fox

Hello Baby!

Illustrated by Steve Jenkins

Beach Lane Books
New York London Toronto Sydney

Hello, baby!

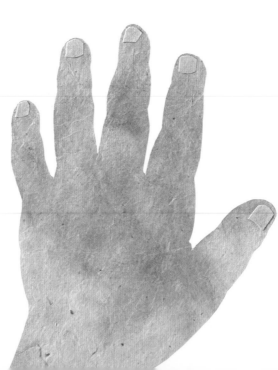

Who are you?

Are you
a monkey
with clever toes?

Perhaps
you're
a porcupine,
twitching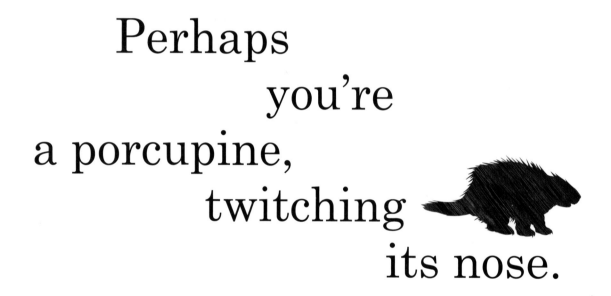
its nose.

Are you an eagle,
     exploring the skies?

Perhaps
you're a gecko
with
rolling eyes.

Are you a lion
              with dust
                        on its paws?

Perhaps you're a hippo with yawning jaws.

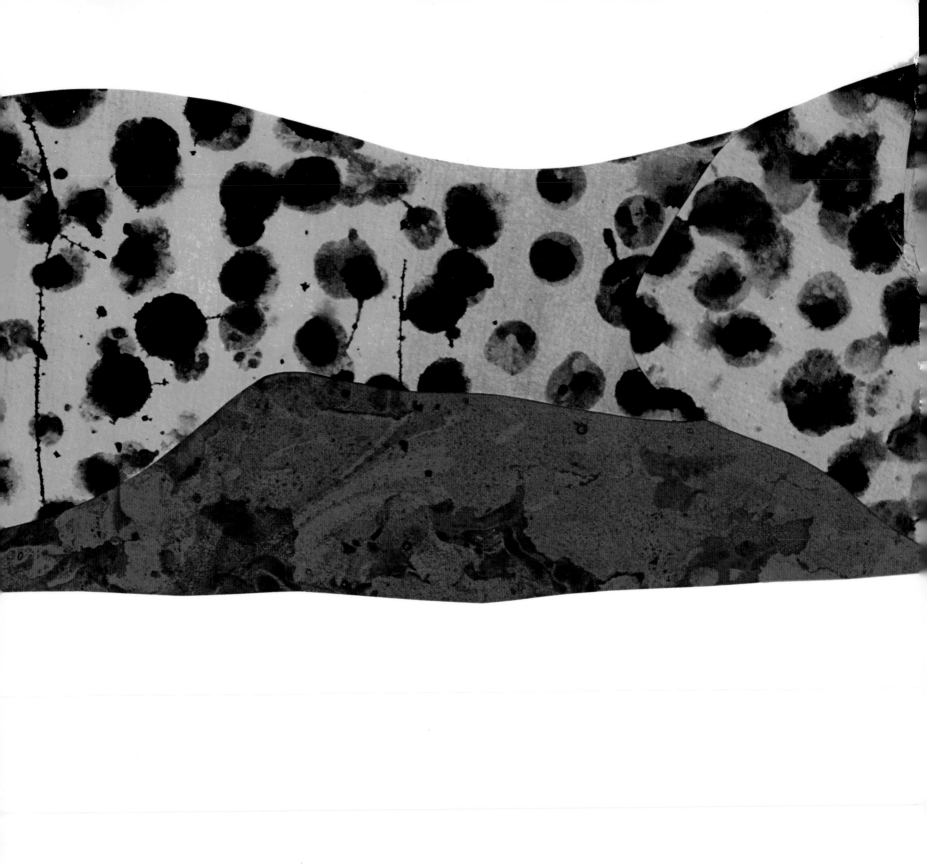

Are you a leopard,
dozing at dusk?

Perhaps you're
an elephant,
wielding a tusk.

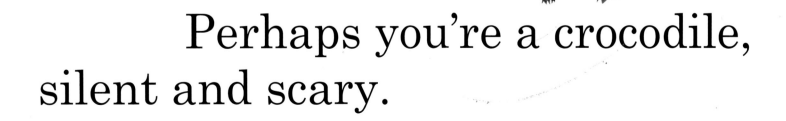

Perhaps you're a crocodile, silent and scary.

Are you a zebra,

sipping a drink?

Perhaps you're an owl
       with a wicked wink.

No?

Then who *are* you, baby?
Wait, let me guess—

Are you a warthog,
hilarious and hairy?

Are you my treasure?
The answer is . . .

Yes!

For Tiwe, Susan, Blessings, and Helen—
my Bulawayo friends
—M. F.

For Jamie
—S. J.

Beach Lane Books
An imprint of Simon & Schuster Children's Publishing Division
1230 Avenue of the Americas, New York, New York 10020
Text copyright © 2009 by Mem Fox
Illustrations copyright © 2009 by Steve Jenkins
The text for this book is set in Century Schoolbook.
The illustrations for this book are rendered in collage.
Manufactured in China
First Edition
2 4 6 8 10 9 7 5 3 1
Library of Congress Cataloging-in-Publication Data
Fox, Mem, 1946–
Hello baby! / Mem Fox ; illustrated by Steve Jenkins. — 1st ed.
p. cm.
Summary: A baby encounters a variety of young animals, including a clever monkey, a hairy warthog,
and a dusty lion cub, before discovering the most precious creature of all.
ISBN: 978-1-4169-8513-6
[1. Stories in rhyme. 2. Babies—Fiction. 3. Animals—Infancy—Fiction.]
I. Jenkins, Steve, 1952– ill. II. Title.
PZ8.3.F8245He 2009
[E]—dc22
2008034421